HORRiD HENRY'S
A-Z of
EVERYTHING
HORRiD

This collection first published in Great Britain in 2011
by Orion Children's Books
a division of the Orion Publishing Group Ltd
Orion House
5 Upper St Martin's Lane
London WC2H 9EA
An Hachette UK Company

1 3 5 7 9 10 8 6 4 2

Compiled by Sally Byford from the *Horrid Henry* books.

The Orion Publishing Group's policy is to use papers that are natural,
renewable and recyclable products and made from wood grown in sustainable forests.
The logging and manufacturing processes are expected to conform to the
environmental regulations of the country of origin.

A catalogue record for this book is available from the British Library.

ISBN 978 1 4440 0226 3

Printed in China

www.orionbooks.co.uk
www.horridhenry.co.uk

Francesca Simon

HORRID HENRY'S
A-Z of
EVERYTHING HORRID

Illustrated by Tony Ross

Orion
Children's Books

Abominable Snowman

Horrid Henry builds an
Abominable Snowman
for the Frosty Freeze
Best Snowman
competition – it's taller
than Henry, with fangs,
hairy scary claws and a
Viking horned helmet.
(See Ballerina Snowgirl,
Best Snowman Competition,
Big Bunny Snowman, Frosty
Freeze Ice Cream Factory)

Acting

Horrid Henry thinks he's the best actor in the world, and that Perfect Peter is a terrible actor who can't sing and squeaks like a squished toad. He can't believe it when Miss Battle-Axe chooses Peter to play Joseph in the school Christmas play. At least he escapes the humiliation of being a blade of grass when he gets the part of the innkeeper.

(See Blade of Grass, Perfect Peter, School Play, Toad)

Aerobic Al

The fastest, sportiest boy in Horrid Henry's class. He loves running, doing push-ups and winning lots of medals and cups. His best friend is Beefy Bert because he's easy to beat at games.

(See Beefy Bert)

6

Ancient Greeks

Henry thinks all they did was just spear each other and eat their children for tea. But they also knew how to win races and deal with unwanted guests.

(See Parthenon)

Angry Anna

A very angry babysitter. When Anna babysits for Horrid Henry, she runs away screaming from the house and Henry's parents have to come home early. She never comes again.

(See Babysitters)

Anxious Andrew

The most anxious boy in Horrid Henry's class. He worries about everything – especially at the swimming class when Henry tells him there's a shark in the pool!

Apples

Horrid Henry hates all fruit and vegetables, but he hates apples most of all. Any grown-up who dares to give Henry an apple on Hallowe'en night had better watch out. Also biting a teeny tiny piece of apple made Henry's first tooth fall out.

(See Fruit, Hallowe'en, Vegetables)

Ashton Athletic

The local football team. Horrid Henry is a big fan, but even when Ashton finally hit the big time and play Manchester United, Henry's mean, horrible, lazy parents don't bother to get him a ticket.

(See Football, Miss Battle-Axe)

Atomic Bunny

Henry gives Peter a scary haircut to turn him into Atomic Bunny for Hallowe'en.

(See Hallowe'en)

Attack-Tack-Tack

An album by the Killer Boy Rats, Henry's top favourite band.

(See Killer Boy Rats)

Baa Baa Sheep Family

Perfect Peter's precious collection of sheep, including Fluff Puff, Lambykins and Squish. He lines them up neatly from biggest to smallest, all five centimetres apart. If one of his sheep has been moved out of place, Peter knows straight away that Henry has been in his bedroom.

(See Collecting, Fluff Puff)

Babbling Bob

The most talkative boy in Horrid Henry's class – he chatters non-stop!

Baby

Perfect Peter hates it when Horrid Henry calls him 'baby' – it's as bad as 'smelly nappy'.

(See Name-Calling, Smelly Nappy, Vomiting Vera)

Babysitters

Horrid Henry hates babysitters – unless they let him stay up all night and eat lots of sweets. He doesn't want an ugly, stuck-up, bossy teenager hanging around all evening, hogging the TV and pigging out on the biscuits. And babysitters don't like Horrid Henry either – after one evening with him, they never come back.

(See Angry Anna, Crabby Chris, Mellow Martin, Rabid Rebecca, Tetchy Tess)

Bad Children's Room

A place where guards take children who misbehave at Our Town Museum.

(See Our Town Museum)

Ballerina Snowgirl

Moody Margaret and Sour Susan build a Ballerina Snowgirl for the Frosty Freeze Best Snowman competition. It's as tall as Margaret, with a big pink tutu wound round its waist.

(See Abominable Snowman, Best Snowman Competition, Big Bunny Snowman, Frosty Freeze Ice Cream Factory)

The Basher

Horrid Henry's newspaper is full of news, gossip and scandal – all invented by Henry. He plans to sell millions of copies, make loads of cold, hard cash and buy a Hip-Hop Robot Dog. When he discovers he's in competition with copycat Moody Margaret's Daily Dagger, he's determined to beat her.

(See Best Boys' Busy Bee, The Daily Dagger, Hip-Hop Robot Dog)

Bathtime

Horrid Henry loves bathtime – making tidal waves and bubble-bath beards, fighting sea monsters and staging battles with Snappy Croc and Yellow Duck. But Dad knows how to spoil a good bath – he makes Henry share with Perfect Peter, who likes the water too cold.

(See Dad, Perfect Peter)

Beans

These slimy green worms are one of Horrid Henry's most hated vegetables – eating them makes him spit and splutter.

(See Vegetables)

Be a Spelling Champion

Horrid Henry loves playing computer games – but not this one. Apart from Beefy Bert who was given Counting Made Easy for Christmas, no one else has such terrible games.

(See Beefy Bert, Computer Games)

Bedrooms

Horrid Henry's bedroom is a pigsty, littered with piles of ripped comics, crumpled sweet wrappers, dirty clothes and broken toys. Peter's bedroom is always clean and tidy, and Henry is forbidden to go in without Peter's permission.

(See Baa Baa Sheep Family,
Perfect Peter)

Bedtime

One of Horrid Henry's most hated words. His bedtime is at eight, with lights out at eight-thirty. Not fair! No one else goes to bed at eight, except Lazy Linda who is always asleep by seven. But Perfect Peter loves settling down at bedtime with a nice story.

(See Lazy Linda, Sammy the Snuggly Snail)

Beefy Bert

The biggest boy in Horrid Henry's class, Bert's answer to everything is "I dunno". His best friend is Aerobic Al.

(See Aerobic Al)

Best Boy

Perfect Peter's favourite magazine, full of top tips for pleasing your parents, and readers' favourite chores.

(See Perfect Peter)

Best Boys' Club

Perfect Peter and his friends Tidy Ted, Spotless Sam and Goody-Goody Gordon hold regular meetings of their Best Boys' Club to discuss all the good deeds they've done that week.

(See Best Boys' Busy Bee, Mottos, Passwords)

Best Boys' Busy Bee

The Best Boys' Club newspaper has exciting features like 'Tidy with Ted', and even a free vegetable chart. Horrid Henry thinks Peter's newspaper should be used in Fluffy's litter tray.

(See The Basher, The Daily Dagger, Fluffy)

Best Boy Magazine

Peter's favourite read tells you how to polish your trophies, and gives Top Tips for pleasing your parents.

Best Friends

Horrid Henry's best friend is Rude Ralph – because they're both rude and horrid. Moody Margaret and Sour Susan are best friends, but only when Susan is doing what she's told, and Margaret isn't being a moody old bossyboots. Perfect Peter's best friends are Tidy Ted, Goody-Goody Gordon and Spotless Sam.

(See Goody-Goody Gordon, Moody Margaret, Perfect Peter, Rude Ralph, Sour Susan, Spotless Sam, Tidy Ted)

Best Snowman Competition

The Frosty Freeze Ice Cream Factory holds a Best Snowman Competition, with a fantastic prize of free ice cream for a year. Horrid Henry, Moody Margaret and Perfect Peter are all desperate to win.

(See Abominable Snowman, Ballerina Snowgirl, Big Bunny Snowman, Frosty Freeze Ice Cream Factory)

Bibble Babble Drink

A black frothy drink which lets you understand people from the future when you time travel. Henry gives one to Peter.

(See Mega-Mean Time Machine)

Big Boppers

One of Horrid Henry's favourite sweets.

(See Sweets)

Big Boss

Horrid Henry's dad's
boss. Henry meets Big
Boss and his son, Bossy
Bill, when he goes to
his dad's work for the
day – and soon finds
himself in big trouble.

(See Bossy Bill, Dad)

Big Bunny Snowman

Perfect Peter's snowman
for the Frosty Freeze Best
Snowman Competition is
a bunny. Henry calls it
a pathetic pimple with
two stones for eyes.

*(See Abominable Snowman,
Ballerina Snowgirl, Best
Snowman Competition, Frosty
Freeze Ice Cream Factory)*

Birthday

Horrid Henry's birthday is in February. His parents dread it every year because Henry demands lots of unsuitable presents and his parties always end in disaster!

(See February, Lazer Zap, Party, Presents)

Biscuits

One of Horrid Henry's favourite snacks, especially Chocolate Fudge Chewies and Triple Choc Chip Marshmallow Chewies. Sometimes his mean, horrible parents don't buy them, but Henry knows where to find a secret supply – Moody Margaret's Secret Club biscuit tin.

(See Hot Chilli Powder Biscuits, Secret Club Tent)

Blade of Grass

The absolute worst part in the School Christmas Play. Only suitable for kids like Weepy William. Great actors like Horrid Henry are destined for bigger roles, like the innkeeper.

(See Acting, School Play, Weepy William)

Blobby Gobbers

One of Horrid Henry's favourite sweets.

(See Sweets)

Blood Boil Bob

Long ago, Blood Boil Bob was a cannibal pirate who turned his younger brother Paul into a shrunken head. Anyone having a Pirate Party risks awakening Blood Boil Bob and his pirate cannibal curse. And anyone whose name begins with 'P' will turn into a shrunken head. At least, that's what Henry tells Perfect Peter when he tries to stop Peter having a Pirate Party.

(See Pirate Party)

Booby Traps

Horrid Henry sets up a brilliant booby trap in the Secret Club tent, using a bucket of water and string, to soak Moody Margaret in cold, muddy water. But funnily enough, Margaret has exactly the same idea to booby trap the Purple Hand Gang den. He also sets traps for Father Christmas.

(See Father Christmas, Purple Hand Gang, Secret Club)

Books

Horrid Henry loves comics, but he loves
TJ Fizz's books too. His favourites
are The Skeleton Skunk series
by TJ Fizz and his worst
book is *The Happy Nappy* by
Milksop Miles.

*(See Comics, Presents, TJ Fizz,
Milksop Miles)*

Book Week

At school Book Week, Horrid Henry's favourite author in the whole
world, TJ Fizz, comes to talk to Henry's class. But Henry is sent out
for eating crisps and ends
up in Miss Lovely's class
instead where the visiting
author is Perfect Peter's
favourite, Milksop
Miles.

*(See Books, Milksop Miles,
TJ Fizz)*

Bookworld

Horrid Henry
beats Clever Clare
in the school reading
competition to win a trip to a theme park! Then he discovers that
the theme park is Bookworld, where you can read to the beat, watch
a thrilling display of speed-reading, and practise checking out library
books. Aaaargh!

Boom-Boom Basher

Horrid Henry is desperate to own a Boom-Boom Basher, a brilliant toy which crashes into everything and has an ear-piercing siren and special trasher attachments.

(See Toys)

Boom-Box

Horrid Henry's CD player, best played at top volume. Ideal for booming the music of the Killer Boy Rats over a quiet, boring campsite, or for helping Henry to concentrate when he's learning his spellings for homework.

(See Camping, Killer Boy Rats)

Bossy Bill

Big Boss, Bill's dad, says that Bill is a great kid, well-behaved, well-mannered, clever, and brilliant at football, maths and the trumpet. Horrid Henry thinks he is one of the yuckiest kids he's ever met – a mean, stuck-up, double-crossing creep, especially when he gets Henry into trouble on 'take your child to work' day.

(See Big Boss)

Boudicca

Miss Battle-Axe's first name.

(See Miss Battle-Axe)

Brainy Brian

The brainiest boy in Horrid Henry's class, he's even as clever as his best friend, Clever Clare. He loves doing puzzles and riddles that no one else can solve.

(See Clever Clare)

Bunny Costume

Perfect Peter's Hallowe'en costume is a big, pink bouncy bunny. Henry is horrified when he realises Mum expects him to go trick or treating with a fluffy pink bunny.

(See Atomic Bunny, Devil Costume, Hallowe'en)

Bunnykins

Perfect Peter's favourite cuddly toy. When Horrid Henry steals Bunnykins from Peter's bedroom, it's war.

Burping

Rude Ralph is a champion burper, Greedy Graham eats too much at parties and burps, and Horrid Henry has a very special burping talent – he can burp to the theme tune of 'Marvin the Maniac'.

(See Greedy Graham, Marvin the Maniac, Rude Ralph)

Cabbage

Horrid Henry hates all vegetables – and cabbage is one of the worst.

(See Vegetables)

Camping

Horrid Henry's parents enjoy going on holiday to a nice, quiet campsite in the countryside with cold showers and lots of fresh air. It's Henry's idea of hell. He wants to stay on a campsite with comfy beds, a heated swimming pool and a giant TV with 57 channels.

(See Boom-Box, Countryside, Holidays)

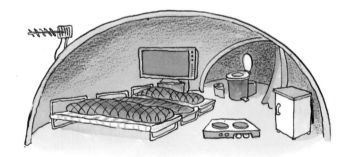

Cannibal Cook

On Horrid Henry's favourite TV cooking programme, chefs compete to see who can cook the most revolting meals.

(See Cooking Cuties, Gourmet Greg, Nibbling Nigel, TV)

Captain Hook

There's always a problem when Horrid Henry and Moody Margaret play at pirates – they both want to be Captain Hook. Until they find something better to do … like making Glop!

(See Glop, Pirate Kit)

Captain of the Football Team

Moody Margaret is the Captain of the Football Team because she's the best and the bossiest footballer in the school.

(See Football, Hot-Foot Henry, Moody Margaret)

Cardigan

One of Horrid Henry's most horrible presents ever is a hideous lime green cardigan from Rich Aunt Ruby. Henry can't believe he has to write a thank you letter for such a terrible present.

(See Presents, Rich Aunt Ruby, Thank You Letters)

Cauliflower Cheese

Horrid Henry can't understand why anyone would want to eat white rubbery blubbery globules of glop.

(See Vegetables)

Chief Spy

Sour Susan is Chief Spy for the Secret Club. She's perfect for the job because she loves telling tales.

(See Sour Susan, Secret Club)

Chips

Horrid Henry loves chips! No wonder 'Gobble and Go' is one of his favourite restaurants – you can eat as many chips as you want.

(See Fat Frank's, Gobble and Go, Restaurant Le Posh, Virtuous Veggie)

Chocolate

One of Horrid Henry's favourite snacks, he spends a lot of his pocket money on chocolate – and the rest goes on sweets, comics and crisps.

(See Biscuits, Packed Lunches, Pocket Money, Sports Day, Sweets)

Chocolate Spitballs

One of Horrid Henry's favourite sweets.

(See Sweets)

Chores

Horrid Henry's weekend is always being ruined because his parents make him do chores. He'd much rather be watching TV and sitting on the comfy black chair. Perfect Peter loves doing chores – he likes helping his parents.

(See Comfy Black Chair, Saturday, Weekend)

Clever Clare

The cleverest girl in Henry's class, Clever Clare always gets top marks at maths and spelling. Clare learned to read when she was two, did longdivision when she was three and built her first telescope when she was five. Her best friend is Brainy Brian because he's clever too.

(See Brainy Brian, Spelling Tests)

Collecting

Horrid Henry and Perfect Peter both enjoy collecting Gizmos from Sweet Tweet cereal packets. Perfect Peter also collects stamps and lovely little sheepies.

(See Baa Baa Sheep Family, Gizmos, Sweet Tweet)

Comfy Black Chair

The best place for watching TV in Horrid Henry's house. Henry and Peter fight every day to sit on the comfy black chair, because the winner gets to decide what to watch on TV, and the loser has to sit on the lumpy sofa.

(See TV)

Comics

Horrid Henry's favourite reading material – especially if it's a Screamin' Demon or Mutant Max comic.

(See Books, TJ Fizz)

Computer

The computer at Horrid Henry's house is only for work – Dad's work, Mum's work and schoolwork. It's NOT for playing silly games … until Henry sets a secret password and takes control.

(See Computer Games)

Computer Games

Horrid Henry's favourite computer games are Intergalactic Robot Rebellion and Snake Master's Revenge III – because he loves zapping aliens and commanding armies. But the only games his mean, horrible parents let him have are Be a Spelling Champion, Virtual Classroom, Name that Vegetable and Whoopee for Numbers.

(See Growing Up)

Cooking Cuties

Cooking Cuties is Perfect Peter's favourite TV cooking programme.

(See Cannibal Cook, TV)

Countryside

Mum, Dad and Perfect Peter love the countryside. Horrid Henry hates it. It's full of dangers like wild beasts, dangerous paths, swollen rivers, stinging nettles, rampaging chickens, quicksand, horrible smells, mud, zombies, vampires, mummies, and worst of all, fresh air.

(See Nature, Walking)

Crabby Chris

A cross and crabby babysitter. When she babysits for Horrid Henry, he hides her homework and pours red grape juice down her new white jeans. She never comes again.

(See Babysitters)

Crisps

Horrid Henry loves salty, crunchy crisps. He can eat them even faster than Greedy Graham. But his mean, horrible parents only allow crisps once a week.

(See Greedy Graham, Vegetables)

Cross Colin

The best man at Pimply Paul and Prissy Polly's wedding, where
Horrid Henry has to be a page boy and carry the gold rings on a
cushion.

(See Page Boy, Pimply Paul, Prissy Polly)

Cross Country Run

This long, sweaty and exhausting race is Horrid Henry's worst event
at school Sports Day − he hates running, but he hates losing too.
So he takes some inspiration from Greek Myths, throws sweets in
Aerobic Al's path, and beats him.

(See Aerobic Al, Sports Day)

Curse of the Mummy Kit

This kit includes a plastic body to
mummify, mummy-wrapping gauze,
a curse book, amulets and removable
mummy organs to put in a canopic jar.
It actually belongs to Perfect Peter,
but Henry's so desperate to get his
hands on it that he turns Peter into a
mummy by wrapping him in loo roll
from head to toe, so Peter can't see him
playing with it.

(See Toys)

Dad

Horrid Henry's dad likes cooking and listening to
classical music. Dad's always telling Henry to turn
down his Boom-Box, but his secret dream is to
be a Rock 'n' Roll god.

(See Boom-Box, Mum, Parents)

Daffy and her Dancing Daisies

Perfect Peter's favourite TV show.
He loves listening to their Greatest Hits
in the car and singing along to
all his favourite songs like
Whoops-a-Daisy, Upsy-Daisy,
and Prance and Dance-a-Daisy.

(See TV)

Dagger

The mark of the Secret Club is a dagger. When Moody Margaret raids the Purple Hand biscuit tin, she leaves behind a dagger drawn on a piece of paper so Henry knows exactly who's outsmarted him.

(See Secret Club)

Daily Dagger

Moody Margaret and Sour Susan's newspaper. They compete on the school playground against Henry's Basher to sell the most copies and buy the first Hip-Hop Robot Dog.

(See The Basher, Best Boys' Busy Bee, Hip-Hop Robot Dog)

Dance Class

Horrid Henry hates being dragged to dance class – he hates the teacher, Miss Impatience Tutu, he hates dancing with other children, and he definitely doesn't want to be a raindrop in the dance class show.

(See Karate, Miss Impatience Tutu, Miss Thumper, Stomping)

De-Bagging

Horrid Henry has started a new craze on the school playground – pulling people's trousers down – which can be very embarrassing if you're wearing frilly pink lacy girls' pants!

(See Underpants)

Devil Costume

Horrid Henry's Hallowe'en costume is red and black with an evil mask, twinkling horns, trident and whippy tail.
He looks great, but Mum expects him to go out with Peter dressed as a fluffy pink bunny.

(See Bunny Costume, Hallowe'en)

Dew Drops

These no-sugar, vegetable-flavoured treats are Perfect Peter's favourite sweets.

(See Sweets)

Diary

Perfect Peter keeps a very boring diary, and when Henry sneaks a peak, he's outraged to discover that Peter doesn't mention him in it once.

Monday
Today I drew a picture of my teacher, Miss Lovely. Miss Lovely gave me a gold star for reading. That's because I'm the best reader in the class. And the best at maths. And the best at everything else.

Tuesday
Today I said please and thank you 236 times

Dirtballs

One of Horrid Henry's favourite sweets.

(See Sweets)

Dirty Dirk

The presenter of Hog House, one of Henry's favourite programmes, in which teenagers compete to win the prize for the most disgusting room.

(See Filthy Final, Hog House)

Dizzy Dave

The dizziest boy in Henry's class. Dizzy Dave likes spinning round like a top, and he's always falling and knocking things over.

(See Sleepovers)

Dr Dettol

Dr Dettol is the doctor in charge on the worst day in the world –
injection day. But ever since Henry bit her, Dr Dettol keeps her
distance!

(See Injections, Nurse Needle)

Dr Jekyll's Spooky Sounds

Stuck-Up Steve hides this in the wardrobe to try and scare Henry.

(See Stuck-Up Steve)

Driller Cannibals

One of Horrid Henry's favourite bands. He plays their songs,
'I'm a can-can-cannibal' and 'Tear down the school' very loudly
on his Boom-Box.

(See Boom-Box)

Duke of Poop

One of Henry's favourite nicknames for Peter.

(See Name-Calling)

NAMES I DON'T WANT
TO BE CALLED
1. Poopsicle
2. Duke of Poop
3. Ugly
4. Nappy face
5. Baby
6. Toad
7. Smelly toad
8. Ugg
9. Worm
10. Wibble pants

Dungeon Drink Kit

This kit contains the recipes and ingredients
for concocting foul-tasting frothy drinks.
Grandma gives Henry a kit just in time for his parents' dinner
party, so one lucky guest gets the chance to taste a horrid potion.
And Henry gets Dungeon-Drinked when Moody Margaret swaps the
Purple Hand Gang's fizzywizz drinks with her own special stinkers.

(See Guests, Mr and Mrs Mossy)

Earnest Ella

A guide at Our Town Museum, who leads torchlight walks down the passage to the past to 'The Wonderful World of Wool' during a school sleepover.

Eerie Eyrie

When Henry plays Gotcha, this is the dragon lair he always wants to buy because everyone who lands on it has to pay a ransom or be eaten. Unfortunately, even when he has it, he never wins because Moody Margaret is a demon Gotcha player.

(See Gotcha)

Enemies

Horrid Henry has lots of enemies and he dreams up horrible ways to defeat them all, like catapulting them into a moat filled with piranha fish, letting crocodiles loose in their bedrooms, or dumping them in snakepits.

(See Bossy Bill, Lisping Lily, Miss Battle-Axe, Moody Margaret, Perfect Peter, Rabid Rebecca, Soggy Sid, Sour Susan, Stuck-up Steve)

Excuses

Horrid Henry is brilliant at making up excuses. At swimming class, he tells Soggy Sid that he's lost his costume or that he has a verruca or a tummy ache. At school he tells Miss Battle-Axe that his homework has been thrown in the recycling box by mistake.

(See Homework, Miss Battle-Axe, Soggy Sid, Swimming,)

Fairies

Henry tricks Peter into climbing a tree at midnight by telling him there are fairies at the bottom of the garden. Peter writes a terrible story called 'Butterfly Fairies Paint the Rainbow'. And Henry doesn't want a fairy on top of the Christmas tree – he wants Terminator Gladiator.

(See Perfect Peter, Terminator Gladiator)

Fang

Horrid Henry's hamster Fang loves sunflower seeds and hates Fluffy the cat. Fang's secret dream is to be bigger than Fluffy.

(See Fluffy)

Fangmanglers

Fangmanglers are the slimiest, scariest, most horrible and frightening monsters in the whole world. They hide in the shadows at night, then sneak out and bite people. Grown-ups never talk about them because they don't want to scare you. That's what Horrid Henry tells everyone anyway.

Fat Frank's

One of Horrid Henry's favourite restaurants.

(See Gobble and Go)

Fate Square

When you land on the Fate Square in Gotcha, you pick up a Fate card. It might tell you to claim a treasure hoard or send you to the Dungeon. The best Fate card of all is when you get to be king for a day and collect rubies from all the other players.

(See Gotcha)

Father Christmas

Henry writes a detailed letter to Father Christmas every year. But he always gets vests, handkerchiefs, books and satsumas instead of the cool presents he's asked for. How hard can it be for Father Christmas to get it right?

(See Presents, Satsumas)

February

Horrid Henry's favourite
month – it's his birthday!
(See Birthday, Party, Presents)

Fiery Fiona

The fieriest girl in
Horrid Henry's class,
she's very cross and
argues a lot.

Filthy Final

The final of Hog House, where the two
filthiest teenagers fight for first prize.
(See Dirty Dirk, Hog House)

Fizzy Fizzers

One of Horrid Henry's many favourite sweets.
(See Sweets)

Fizzywizz

Horrid Henry's best fizzy drink.
It's perfect for celebrating a Purple Hand Gang
victory over the Secret Club – unless Moody
Margaret has already sneaked in and swapped
their fizzywizz for Dungeon Drinks.
*(See Dungeon Drink Kit, Purple Hand Gang, Secret
Club)*

Fluff Puff

Fluff Puff, with its pink and yellow nose, is Perfect Peter's favourite sheep from his lovely little sheepies collection.

(See Baa Baa Sheep Family)

Fluffy

Horrid Henry's family cat, Fluffy, is big, fat and white. She loves sleeping, hates moving about, and her secret dream is to live in a house filled with mice.

(See Fang)

Foam Teeth

One of Horrid Henry's best sweets.

(See Sweets)

Football

Horrid Henry likes to think he's the best footballer in the class. But although he's good at pushing, shoving and tripping, he isn't actually very good at playing football. Unfortunately for Henry, Moody Margaret is the best footballer in the class. Not only that, she's the second best player and the third best player too.

(See Ashton Athletic, Captain of the Football Team, Hot-Foot Henry, Moody Margaret)

Fort

The Purple Hand Gang's den is hidden behind some carefully placed prickly branches – perfect for spying on Moody Margaret's Secret Club.
(See Purple Hand Gang, Secret Club)

Frosty Freeze Ice Cream Factory

A school visit to the Frosty Freeze Ice Cream Factory would be Horrid Henry's ideal trip. The factory's delicious flavours include Chunky Chocolate Fab Fudge Caramel Delight, Vanilla Whip Tutti-Fruitti Toffee Treat, and Triple Fudge Gooey Chocolate Chip Peanut Butter Marshmallow Custard. Every year, Frosty Freeze holds a snowman competition, and the winner gets a year's supply of ice cream.

(See Abominable Snowman, Ballerina Snowgirl, Best Snowman Competition, Big Bunny Snowman, Our Town Museum, School Trip)

Fruit

Horrid Henry hates fruit, especially apples.

(See Apples, Satsumas)

Gappy Nappy

A character in the book
The Happy Nappy, written by
Milksop Miles. Gappy Nappy
is always wailing, 'I'm leaking!'
(See The Happy Nappy, Milksop Miles)

Ghost Quest

A book written by Horrid Henry's favourite author.

(See TJ Fizz)

Ghouls' Jewels

Another book by Horrid Henry's top author.

(See TJ Fizz)

Gizmos

Horrid Henry and Perfect Peter eat box after box of Sweet Tweet to get the free Gizmos for their collections. There are ten different coloured Gizmos to collect, from the common green to the rare gold.

(See Collecting, Hobbies, Sweet Tweet, Twizzle Cards)

Glop

A yucky mixture made from all sorts of stuff in the kitchen. Horrid Henry and Moody Margaret make Glop and dare each other to eat it. And when Perfect Peter comes along feeling hungry, isn't it lucky that there's plenty left?

Gobble and Go

Horrid Henry's favourite restaurant in the whole wide world. Its motto is 'The chips just keep on coming!' Gobble and Go serves jumbo burgers, huge pizzas, lakes of ketchup and fifty-two flavours of ice cream. Best of all, there are no vegetables, and each table has its own TV.

(See Chips, Ice Cream, Ketchup, Pizza, Vegetables)

Good as Gold Book

The Good as Gold Book records how many stars each of the children at school have been awarded. Perfect Peter always has the most.

(See Perfect Peter)

Goody-Goody Gordon

One of Perfect Peter's best friends, and a member of the Best Boys' Club.

(See Best Boys' Club)

Gooey Chewies

One of Horrid Henry's yummiest best sweets.

(See Sweets)

Goo-Shooter

The Goo-Shooter splatters green goo over everything and everybody. Horrid Henry wants one.

(See Goo-Shooter World, Gross-Out, Mega-Whirl Goo Shooter, Toys)

Goo-Shooter World

A brilliant place for a party. What rotten luck that Rude Ralph has his birthday party at Goo-Shooter World the very same day that Henry has to go with his parents to Vomiting Vera's christening.

(See Goo-Shooter, Vomiting Vera)

Gorgeous Gurinder

The most beautiful girl in Horrid Henry's class.
Gurinder is not very good at concentrating
because she spends a lot of time gazing at
her reflection in the mirror. She always looks
lovely, except when Moody Margaret gives her
a Magnificent Makeover and she looks as if a
paint pot has been poured down her cheeks.
(See Makeovers)

Gotcha

Horrid Henry's favourite board game.
You choose a gargoyle, a skull or a claw as
your piece. The aim of the game is to buy dragon lairs, like Eerie Eyrie,
Rocky Ravine and Vulture Valley, and collect lots of rubies.
Henry likes being the banker so he can steal money from the bank
when none of the other players are looking.
(See Eerie Eyrie, Fate Square, Rocky Ravine, Vulture Valley)

Gourmet Greg

A chef who appears on the TV programme, Cannibal Cook.
His best dish is lizard eyes in custard.

(See Cannibal Cook, Nibbling Nigel)

Grandma

Horrid Henry's mum's mum.
Henry loves it when Grandma
visits, because she always
brings great presents, like the
Tyrannosaur Dinosaur Roars.

(See Presents, Snappy Zappy Critter,
Tyrannosaur Dinosaur Roars)

Grandpa

Horrid Henry's dad's dad.
Grandpa likes smoking
his pipe and snoozing,
sometimes at the same
time – with disastrous
results.

Granny

Horrid Henry's dad's mum. Granny really annoys Henry's parents
at Christmas when they're cooking lunch by telling them they're
doing everything wrong.

Greasy Greta,
the Demon Dinner Lady

A gigantic dinner lady at Horrid Henry's school with piggy eyes and fat wobbly cheeks. She waddles between the tables, snatching all the best treats and sweets from the pupils. Until Henry comes up with a plan to stop her once and for all . . .

(See Hot Chilli Powder Biscuits)

Great-Aunt Greta

Horrid Henry and Perfect Peter have never met Great-Aunt Greta, but they know she is very old. She thinks Henry is a little girl called Henrietta and sends him presents like underpants and dolls, and she thinks Peter is a teenager and sends him cool stuff like money, a football and a computer game.

(See De-bagging, Underpants, Walkie-Talkie-Burpy-Slurpy-Teasy-Weasy-Doll

Greedy Graham

The greediest boy in Horrid Henry's class. Greedy Graham's favourite snacks are crisps, chocolate and sweets.

(See Shop 'n' Drop, Sleepovers)

Grisly Ghoul Grub Box

Horrid Henry is the proud owner of a Grisly Ghoul Grub Box. It makes horrible snacks like Rotten Crispies and Nasty Nuts – perfect for scaring away unwanted dinner guests.

(See Mr and Mrs Mossy)

Gross-Out

Horrid Henry loves this TV programme with its cherry pie and ice-cream-eating contests and its goo-shooting shoot-outs. He's even a member of the Gross-Out Fan Club, and his dream comes true when he gets invited to go on the show.

(See Goo-Shooter, Marvin the Maniac, Tank Thomas and Tapioca Tina, TV)

Grow and Show

A TV show for tinies, all about vegetables – it's one of Perfect Peter's top favourites.

(See TV)

Growing Up

Henry has lots of different career ideas. He wants to earn a million pounds a week testing computer games. He wants to be a chef and open a chain of restaurants called 'Henry's! Where the eatin' can't be beaten!' He's also going to be Monsieur Henri, a hairdresser who gives scary haircuts, rule the world as King Henry the Horrible, and be a famous author.

(See Computer Games, King Henry the Horrible)

Guests

Horrid Henry's parents don't have guests very often, as something always goes wrong if Henry's around. But Perfect Peter knows that guests come first and he always minds his manners.

(See Dungeon Drink Kit, Grisly Ghoul Grub Box, Manners, Mr and Mrs Mossy)

Hairy Hellhounds

One of Horrid Henry's favourite bands.

Hallowe'en

Henry's favourite kind of day – entirely devoted to stuffing his face with sweets and playing horrid tricks.

(See Atomic Bunny, Bunny Costume, Devil Costume)

Hankie

Perfect Peter always uses a hankie and never picks his nose. Horrid Henry thinks a sleeve works much better.

(See Manners)

The Happy Nappy

Perfect Peter's favourite book by Milksop Miles, about the adventures of a group of giant nappies – Rappy Nappy, Zappy Nappy, Tappy Nappy and Gappy Nappy. Horrid Henry thinks it's the dumbest book ever.

(See Books, Book Week, Gappy Nappy, Milksop Miles)

The Happy Nappy Song

Horrid Henry hates the stupid Happy Nappy Song.

> Oh I'm a happy nappy,
> A happy zappy nappy
> I wrap up your bottom, snug and tight,
> And keep you dry all through the night.
> Oh, oh . . .

(See The Happy Nappy, Milksop Miles)

59

Happy Shopper Supermarket

Horrid Henry hates heaving his heavy bones round the Happy Shopper Supermarket. His mum always buys boring things like toothpaste, spinach and socks. There's only one thing worse – and that's shopping for clothes.

(See Shopping)

Head Teacher

Horrid Henry's head teacher is Mrs Oddbod. If Henry were the head teacher instead, he'd have assemblies about the best TV programmes, competitions for gruesome grub recipes and speed-eating contests.

(See Mrs Oddbod)

Helpful Hari

A friend of Perfect Peter's who gets invited to his Pirate Party.

(See Pirate Party)

Hip-Hop Robot Dog

According to Henry, everyone has the exciting new dancing toy, the Hip-Hop Robot Dog, except for him. But his mean, horrible parents say it's too expensive and too noisy, so Henry comes up with a great idea to make some money – by writing and selling his own newspaper.

(See The Basher, Daily Dagger, Presents, Toys)

Hobbies

Horrid Henry's hobbies are watching TV, reading comics, stuffing his face with sweets and crisps, and collecting Gizmos.

(See Comics, Crisps, Gizmos, Sweets, TV)

Hog House

One of Horrid Henry's favourite TV game shows, presented by Dirty Dirk, in which Filthy Phil, Mouldy Myra and Tornado Tariq compete to have the most disgusting room and reach the Filthy Final.

(See Dirty Dirk, Filthy Final)

Holidays

Horrid Henry's idea of a great holiday is sitting on the sofa eating crisps and watching TV. His parents have different ideas, like visiting museums or castles, or camping.

(See Camping)

Homework

Miss Battle-Axe loves giving homework. Horrid Henry hates doing it.

He has much better things to do with his time, like playing computer games or watching TV and eating crisps. Henry makes up some special homework just for Bossy Bill (Five Reasons Why Watching TV is Better Than Reading.)

(See Bossy Bill, Miss Battle-Axe)

The Hoppy Hippo

One of Perfect Peter's favourite books.

Horrid Henry!

Lord High Excellent Majesty
of the Universe.

*(See EVERYTHING in this utterly
wicked A-Z.)*

Horrid Henry, Il Stupendioso

The greatest magician ever. In the school talent show, Horrid Henry, Il Stupendioso, is sure he's going to win the chance to appear on TV in Talent Tigers. He's going to perform the greatest trick the world has ever seen … he's going to wake the dead…

(See Talent Tigers)

Hot Chilli Powder Biscuits

Horrid Henry's secret biscuit recipe – a shock in store for a greedy snack snatcher.

(See Greasy Greta the Demon Dinner Lady)

Hot-Foot Henry

In his daydreams, Henry is Hot-Foot Henry, spectacular goal-scorer, man of the match, the greatest footballer who's ever lived.

(See Captain of the Football Team, Football)

Ice Cream

Horrid Henry could live on ice cream, but his mean, horrible parents don't let him have it very often. And when they do, Henry isn't even allowed to put on his own hot fudge sauce, whipped cream or sprinkles.

(See Frosty Freeze Ice Cream Factory, Gobble and Go, Sleepovers)

Injections

The only thing in the world that Henry is scared of. In fact he can barely even say the word! So when Nurse Needle chooses the longest, sharpest, most wicked needle for Henry, he quickly thinks up a cunning plan to escape...

(See Dr Dettol, Nurse Needle)

Inky Ian

The inkiest boy in Horrid Henry's class – Ian is always covered in ink. He was inspired by the writer, Ian Rankin.

Intergalactic Robot Rebellion

One of Henry's favourite computer games.

(See Computer Games)

Intergalactic Samurai Gorillas

These toy gorillas launch real stinkbombs – and Horrid Henry wants one.

(See Stinkbombs)

Jazzy Jim

The best musician in Horrid Henry's class, Jazzy Jim plays the drums and turns any flat surface into an instrument. He shouts 'Be Bop-a-lu-la' a lot and bounces around to the beat.

Jolly Josh

The jolliest boy in Horrid Henry's class, Josh is always cheerful and likes playing practical jokes on people.

Jumpy Jeffrey

Jeffrey is the jumpiest boy in Miss Impatience Tutu's Dance Class. Horrid Henry is always treading on his toes.

(See Dance Class, Miss Impatience Tutu)

Karate

Horrid Henry wants to go to karate classes instead of dance class. Then he won't be so scared of Kung-Fu Kate, who is training to be a black belt.

(See Dance Class, Kung-Fu Kate)

Ketchup

One of Horrid Henry's favourite foods.

(See Gobble and Go, Vegetables)

Killer Boy Rats

Horrid Henry's best band. He has all three of their albums – Attack-Tack-Tack, Manic Panic, and Splat! and he plays them very loudly on his Boom-Box. His favourite song goes like this:

I'm dead, you're dead, we're dead
Get over it.
Dead is great, dead's where it's at
'cause . . .

(See Attack-Tack-Tack, Boom-Box, Manic Panic, Splat!)

King Henry the Horrible

When Henry is king of the world, he'll be King Henry the Horrible. He'll have three TVs in every room, eat sweets for dinner, and make it a law that parents, not children have to go to school. Anyone who dares to say the word 'homework' will be thrown to the crocodiles.

(See Growing Up, Homework, TV)

Knight Fight

Horrid Henry loves watching the two knights battle it out in this TV show.

(See TV)

Kung-Fu Kate

Kung-Fu Kate is the scariest girl in Horrid Henry's class because she's a martial arts champion.

(See Karate)

Lazer Zap

A brilliant place for a
birthday party – everyone
dresses up as spacemen and
blasts each other in dark
tunnels. Horrid Henry causes
so much trouble there at
Tough Toby's party, that
when he wants to have
his own party at Lazer
Zap, his parents
discover he's been
banned forever.

(See Birthday, Tough Toby)

Lazy Linda

The laziest girl in Horrid Henry's class. She loves sleeping and is often caught snoring in class.

(See Bedtime)

Lisping Lily

New Nick's little sister. Horrid Henry first meets her when he goes for a sleepover at Nick's. Lily is always following Henry around – she wants him to give her a big kiss and to marry her!

(See New Nick, Sleepovers)

Lord High Excellent Majesty of the Purple Hand

Horrid Henry's title as leader of the Purple Hand Gang.

(See Purple Hand Gang, Lord Worm)

Lord Worm

Perfect Peter's title in the Purple Hand Gang. Henry later promotes him to Lord High Worm.

(See Purple Hand Gang, Lord High Excellent Majesty of the Purple Hand)

Lydia

Miss Lovely's first name.

(See Miss Lovely)

Mad Machines

A book by Henry's favourite author, TJ Fizz.

(See TJ Fizz)

Mad Moon Madison

The crazy drummer for the Mouldy Drumsticks, one of Henry's best bands.

(See Mouldy Drumsticks)

Magic Martha

A girl in Henry's class –
she's brilliant at magic tricks.

Makeovers

Horrid Henry thinks Margaret's Magnificent Makeovers are stupid –
until he discovers that Margaret is actually making money. Then he
sets up his own Marvellous Makeovers, and gets to work – with some
scary results.

(See Gorgeous Gurinder)

Manic Panic

An album by the Killer Boy Rats, Henry's favourite band.

(See Killer Boy Rats)

Manners

Perfect Peter always remembers to say 'please' and 'thank you' unlike Henry. So imagine Peter's delight when he's invited to be a special guest on the TV show, Manners With Maggie.

(See Hankie, Manners With Maggie)

Manners With Maggie

One of Perfect Peter's favourite TV programmes. The presenter, Maggie, shows how to hold a knife and fork elegantly, how to fold a hankie perfectly, and how to eat soup without slurping. Maggie is horrified when she meets Horrid Henry – a boy who wipes his nose on his sleeve, eats dessert before the main course and eats with his fingers.

(See Hankie, Manners)

Marvin the Maniac

The presenter of Gross-Out, one of Horrid Henry's favourite TV shows.

(See Gross-Out)

Mega-Mean Time Machine

Horrid Henry's time-travelling machine made from the new washing machine box. Henry travels back and forth in time – and plays his greatest trick ever on Perfect Peter.

(See Bibble Babble Drink)

Mega-Whirl Goo-Shooter

Even better than an ordinary Goo-Shooter, the Mega-Whirl Goo-Shooter sprays fluorescent goo for fifty metres in every direction.

(See Goo-Shooter)

Mellow Martin

Martin is the most laidback babysitter ever, but even he says he's busy when he's asked to babysit Henry for a second time.

(See Babysitters)

Milksop Miles

The author of Perfect Peter's favourite book, *The Happy Nappy*. Milksop Miles loves doing school visits, playing his guitar and organising jolly sing-songs.
(See Books, Book Week, The Happy Nappy, TJ Fizz)

Mini Minnie

A little friend of Perfect Peter's who gets invited to his Pirate Party.
(See Pirate Party)

Miss Battle-Axe

Henry's scary teacher. She hates children, never smiles and always keeps her beady eyes on Horrid Henry. She likes history and giving loads of homework. When she isn't at school, she's a secret supporter of Ashton Athletic, the local football team. She declares herself Man of the Match during the lunchtime game between Aerobic Al's team and Moody Margaret's. Henry would like to see her zapped into outer space to work in alien salt mines.
(See Ashton Athletic, Boudicca, Homework, School)

Miss Impatience Tutu

The Dance Class teacher is skinny and bony, with long stringy grey hair, a sharp nose, pointy elbows and knobbly knees. No one has ever seen her smile. Perhaps this is because Miss Tutu hates teaching, noise and children, especially Horrid Henry.

(See Dance Class)

Miss Lovely

Perfect Peter's teacher. Miss Lydia Lovely is the best teacher ever. Kind and fun – she makes learning a joy. Peter's secret dream is to marry her.

(See Lydia, Teachers)

Miss Marvel

Horrid Henry's first ever teacher, who Henry sent screaming from the classroom after only two weeks.

(See Teachers)

Miss Thumper

The plump pianist at Miss Impatience Tutu's Dance Class who bangs on the piano keys for the classes and the dance shows.

(See Dance Class, Miss Impatience Tutu)

Money

Horrid Henry loves money – especially spending it, which is why he doesn't have any. His mean, horrible relatives never give him enough money for his birthday or Christmas, so Henry is always thinking up money-making schemes, like selling Peter as a slave or writing his own newspaper.

(See The Basher, Pocket Money, Skeleton Bank)

Moody Margaret

The moodiest girl in Horrid Henry's class, Leader of the Secret Club, Captain of the Football Team, Sour Susan's best friend (sometimes), demon Gotcha player, Horrid Henry's next-door neighbour and worst enemy. Margaret hates boys and loves being the boss. She has better toys than Horrid Henry and a tree house. She plays the trumpet, very loudly and very early in the morning, and screams, very often and very loudly. Her mum calls her My Little Maggie Moo and My Little Maggie Muffin.

(See Captain Hook, Captain of the Football Team, Gotcha, Pirate Kit, Secret Club, Sleepovers, Sour Susan, Screaming)

Mottos

Every club needs a good motto. Horrid Henry's Purple Hand motto is: 'Down with girls', Moody Margaret's Secret Club motto is 'Down with boys' and Perfect Peter's Best Boys' Club's motto is 'Can I help?'
(See Best Boys' Club, Purple Hand Gang, Secret Club)

Mouldy Drumsticks

One of Henry's best bands.

Mr and Mrs Mossy

Mrs Mossy is Henry's mum's new boss at work. Horrid Henry calls her Mrs Bossy. When Henry's mum invites Mr and Mrs Mossy to dinner, Henry gobbles up all the crisps and replaces them with Rotten Crispies from his Grisly Ghoul Grub Box. Luckily for him, it's Perfect Peter's job to serve the guests . . .

(See Guests, Grisly Ghoul Grub Box)

Mr Kill

Horrid Henry's teddy. Henry whacks Mr Kill on the bedpost every time he walks past. He'd never admit it, he can't sleep without his teddy.

Mr Ninius Nerdon

The toughest, meanest, nastiest teacher in the school, nicknamed Nerdy Nerd by Horrid Henry. When he teaches their class, Henry bets Ralph that he can make Mr Nerdon run out screaming by the end of lunchtime. But Mr Nerdon really is one tough teacher.

(See Teachers)

Mrs Battle-Axe

Miss Battle-Axe's mum. Mrs Battle-Axe is even taller, skinnier and more ferocious than her daughter. Horrid Henry is amazed to see her nagging Miss Battle-Axe about her table manners at Restaurant Le Posh – he didn't realise that teachers ever left school, let alone had mums.

(See Miss Battle-Axe)

Mrs Oddbod

The Head Teacher at Henry's school. She's well-known for wittering on about hanging up coats, not running in the corridors, and walking down staircases on the right.

(See Head Teacher)

Mrs Zip

One of Horrid Henry's teachers – Horrid Henry had her running screaming from the classroom after just one day, even quicker than Miss Marvel!

(See Miss Marvel)

Muesli

Horrid Henry hates muesli nearly as much as he hates vegetables. All those healthy cereals, raisins and currants. Bleccch!

(See Vegetables)

Mum

Mum loves walking in the country, hates cooking, and her secret dream is to be a tap dancer. She wishes Horrid Henry was polite, tidy and helpful, like Perfect Peter. She tries hard to make Henry eat vegetables, but when nobody's looking, she sneaks sweets from the sweet jar.

(See Countryside, Perfect Peter)

Mummies

Henry loves mummies. What could be more thrilling than an ancient, wrapped-up dead body? No wonder he wants to get his hands on Perfect Peter's Curse of the Mummy Kit.

(See Curse of the Mummy Kit)

Mutant Max

One of Horrid Henry's favourite comics.

(See Comics)

Nappy Pants

One of Henry's most horrible names for Perfect Peter.

(See Name-Calling)

Name That Vegetable

Horrid Henry's parents are happy for him to play this computer game, but Henry would much rather be zapping aliens than naming vegetables.

(See Computer Games)

Name-Calling

Horrid Henry has lots of horrible names for Perfect Peter. Some are short like 'worm' and 'toad' and some are long like 'telltale frogface ninnyhammer toady poo bag'! He also has horrible names for Moody Margaret like 'moody old grouch' and 'old pants face'.

(See Moody Margaret, Perfect Peter)

Nasty Nuts

One of the revolting snacks that Henry makes with his Grisly Ghoul Grub Box.

(See Grisly Ghoul Grub Box)

Nature

Perfect Peter loves nature and nature programmes, and longs for a nature kit for Christmas. Horrid Henry hates nature – it smells!

(See Countryside)

Needy Neil

The neediest boy in Horrid Henry's school, and Weepy William's younger brother. Needy Neil wants his mum to sit next to him in class.

Nellie's Nursery

One of Perfect Peter's favourite TV programmes, all about creatures with big bellies who eat purple jellies at Nellie's Nursery.

(See TV)

New Nick

The newest boy in Horrid Henry's class. He has a sister called Lisping Lily and his mum and dad have an opera club and five enormous black dogs. Their house is very noisy and very messy – it's too noisy and messy even for Horrid Henry, and when he goes for a sleepover with New Nick, he can't wait to get home.

(See Lisping Lily, Sleepovers)

Nibbling Nigel

A chef on the TV programme, Cannibal Cook. His best dish is jellied worm soufflé.

(See Cannibal Cook, Gourmet Greg)

Nits

Nits love Horrid Henry's hair – they gather from far and wide to have parties on his head. But Henry thinks it's only fair to spread the nits around his classmates. Why should they escape Nitty Nora's beastly bug-busting combs?

(See Nitty Nora)

Nitty Nora

Nitty Nora Bug Explorer is the Nit Nurse who comes to Henry's school. She terrifies the pupils with her ferocious combs and other instruments of torture.

(See Nits)

Nose Pickers

One of Horrid Henry's favourite sweets.

(See Sweets)

Nudie Foodie

A celebrity chef who introduces healthy meals at Henry's school.

Nunga Nu

The Secret Club password. When a Secret Club member wants to enter the tent, they say 'Nunga', and anyone inside answers back, 'Nunga Nu'.

(See Passwords, Secret Club)

Nurse Needle

The nurse on duty on injection day. Ever since Henry kicked her, Nurse Needle has known he's trouble, so she chooses the longest, sharpest needle when it's his turn for an injection.

(See Dr Dettol, Injections)

Our Town Museum

The town museum is a boring old dump. Its exhibitions include
Mr Jones's collection of rubber bands, soil from Miss Montague's garden
and the Mayor's baby pictures. Henry would much rather visit the
Frosty Freeze Ice Cream Factory.

(See Frosty Freeze Ice Cream Factory, School Trip)

Packed Lunches

Horrid Henry's ideal lunch is four packets of crisps, chocolate, doughnuts, cake, lollies – and just one grape so he can tell his parents he's eaten some fruit – all packed inside his Terminator Gladiator lunchbox. But with Greasy Greta the Demon Dinner Lady around, he has to keep a close eye on his goodies.

(See Greasy Greta the Demon Dinner Lady, Terminator Gladiator)

Page Boy

Horrid Henry doesn't want to be a page boy at Prissy Polly and Pimply Paul's wedding. He has to wear a lilac ruffled shirt, green satin knickerbockers, tights, a pink cummerbund and pointy white satin shoes with gold buckles.

(Cross Colin, Pimply Paul, Prissy Polly)

Pancakes

Horrid Henry loves the smell of pancakes. They're his favourite breakfast – with lashings of maple syrup. But he's not so keen on country pancakes (because it's just another name for cowpats)!

(See Countryside)

Parents

Horrid Henry thinks his parents are the meanest, most horrible parents in the whole world. He wonders when his real parents, the King and Queen, are going to come and take him away to the palace where he can do exactly what he wants.

(See Dad, Mum)

Parthenon

A group project on the Ancient Greeks. Henry has to build it out of loo rolls and cardboard.

(See Ancient Greeks)

Party

Horrid Henry would love to have a Lazer Zap party, like Tough Toby, or a Pirate Party, until Perfect Peter has one, because Henry can't possibly have the same party as his wormy little brother. But really the whole point of a party is just to get loads of presents.

(See Lazer Zap, Pirate Party, Presents)

Passwords

Every club needs a secret password to prevent enemies getting into their den. The Purple Hand Gang's password is 'Smelly Toads', the Secret Club's password is 'Nunga Nu', and the Best Boys' Club's password is 'Vitamins'.

(See Best Boys' Club, Nunga Nu, Purple Hand Gang, Secret Club)

Perfect Peter

Horrid Henry's little brother. Perfect Peter is perfect, tidy and polite and always eats all his vegetables. He likes reading quietly, playing the cello, and helping his mum and dad. His secret dream is to marry Miss Lovely.

(See Bedrooms, Bedtime, Chores, Good as Gold Book, Name-Calling)

Perky Parveen

One of Perfect Peter's friends who is invited to his Pirate Party.

(See Pirate Party)

Pimply Paul

Married to Horrid Henry's cousin, Prissy Polly, and father of Vomiting Vera. His face is covered in huge spots. He calls Henry a brat and has never forgiven him for spoiling his wedding.

(See Prissy Polly, Vomiting Vera)

Pirate Kit

Horrid Henry sometimes plays with Moody Margaret, but only because she has a complete pirate kit – hook, cutlass, sword, dagger, eye patch, plumed hat, and skull and crossbones.

(See Captain Hook)

Pirate Party

When Perfect Peter has a Pirate Party, complete with pirate outfits, skull and crossbones flags, and a treasure hunt, Henry is furious. It was his idea first – so he scares Peter by telling him all about Blood Boil Bob and the pirate cannibal curse.

(See Blood Boil Bob)

Pizza

One of Horrid Henry's favourite foods, the bigger the better.

(See Chips, Gobble and Go)

Plughole Monster

A monster who sneaks up the drain while you're having a bath, slithers through the plughols and sucks children down. Henry invents him to scare Peter.

Pocket Money

Mum and Dad give Horrid Henry 50p a week, but it's never enough for all the sweets, toys and comics that Henry needs to buy. Rude Ralph gets a pound a week! Perfect Peter is happy with 30p a week and he always saves loads. He says, 'if you look after the pennies, the pounds will look after themselves.'

(See Chocolate, Comics, Skeleton Bank, Sweets, Toys)

Dear old wrinkly Mum
Don't be glum
Cause you've got a fat tum
And an even bigger bum
Ho ho ho hum
Love from your son,

Henry

Poems

Horrid Henry hates writing poems. Even the word 'poem' makes him want to throw up. But at Christmas, Henry realises that poems make great presents — they're quick to write and, best of all, so cheap!

Pongy Poo Poo

One of Henry's nastiest names for Perfect Peter.

(See Name-Calling)

Poopsicle

Another of Henry's nasty names for Peter.

(See Name-Calling)

Presents

Horrid Henry always writes long present lists of brilliant toys, but his mean old parents and Father Christmas always get him something really boring, like an encyclopaedia, a satsuma, or socks. His worst presents include a cardigan, a fountain pen, vests and pants, a tapestry kit and a book called 'Cook Your Own Healthy Nutritious Food'.

(See Cardigan, Father Christmas, Grandma, Satsumas, Socks, Toys)

Prissy Polly

Horrid Henry's cousin, married to
Pimply Paul and mother of Vomiting
Vera. Henry doesn't like Polly because
she's always squeaking and squealing.
(See Page Boy, Pimply Paul, Vomiting Vera)

Purple Hand Gang

Horrid Henry's club – and the best
club ever. No girls are allowed.
Moody Margaret's stupid Secret
Club is the sworn enemy.
*(See Fort, Lord High Excellent Majesty
of the Purple Hand, Lord Worm, Mottos,
Passwords, Rude Ralph, Secret Club)*

Purple Hand Throne

The throne for the Lord High Excellent
Majesty of the Purple Hand Gang.
*(See Lord High Excellent Majesty of the Purple
Hand Gang, Purple Hand Gang)*

Queen

There's great excitement at Horrid Henry's school when the Queen comes to visit, and Perfect Peter is chosen to present her with a bouquet. Henry tricks Peter by telling him that if he greets the Queen the wrong way, he'll get his head chopped off.

Rabid Rebecca

The toughest teen in town. Rabid Rebecca
is one mean babysitter. She sent Rude Ralph
to bed at six o'clock, made Tough Toby get
into his pyjamas at five o'clock and do all his
homework, and ordered Moody Margaret
to wash the floor. But she's no match for
Horrid Henry . . .

*(See Babysitters, Moody Margaret, Rude Ralph,
Tough Toby)*

Rapper Zapper

One of Horrid Henry's favourite TV shows, Rapper Zapper zips around
in outer space, defeating aliens.

(See TV)

Restaurant Le Posh

The best French restaurant in town, with snowy-white tablecloths, yellow silk chairs and huge gold chandeliers. The food is posh – so definitely no burgers, chips or pizza. When Rich Aunt Ruby takes Henry and his family there, Henry discovers a new favourite food...

(See Rich Aunt Ruby, Snails)

Rich Aunt Ruby

Horrid Henry's mum's sister and mother to Stuck-up Steve. Rich Aunt Ruby is rich and posh, and she lives in a big, old house. Her favourite restaurant is Restaurant Le Posh, and her secret dream is to be best friends with the Queen.

(See Queen, Restaurant Le Posh, Stuck-up Steve)

Robot Rebels

One of Horrid Henry's favourite TV shows.

(See TV)

Rocky Ravine

One of the best squares to buy in the great game of Gotcha.

(See Gotcha)

Roller Bowlers

Trainers on wheels with lots of
different sound effects to
choose from, like Sonic Boom,
Screech, Fire-Engine,
Drums, Canon and Siren.
You can hear them from
miles away.

Root-a-Toot Trainers

Trainers with red lights that
flash every time your feet hit
the floor. Henry loves his
pair of Root-a-Toot trainers,
especially the earsplitting
bugle blast that shakes the
house and makes Dad cover
his ears.

(See Shopping)

Rotten Crispies

Horrid Henry makes these revolting snacks with his Grisly Ghoul
Grub Box, and tricks Perfect Peter into serving them to Mum and
Dad's dinner guests.

(See Grisly Ghoul Grub Box, Mr and Mrs Mossy)

Rubber Blubbers

One of Horrid Henry's favourite sweets.

(See Sweets)

Rude Ralph

Horrid Henry's best friend,
member of the Purple Hand
Gang, and champion burper.
Rude Ralph is always
saying rude words and he
never says 'please', 'thank
you', 'sorry'
or 'you're welcome'.
*(See Best Friends, Burping,
Manners, Purple Hand Gang)*

Sammy the Snail

One of Perfect Peter's favourite TV shows.

(See TV)

Sammy the Snuggly Snail

Perfect Peter's favourite bedtime book. It's not at all scary!

(See Bedtime, Slimy the Slug)

Satsumas

Every year, Horrid Henry finds satsumas in his Santa's sack. Doesn't Father Christmas understand? Satsumas are NOT presents, satsumas are fruit, and Horrid Henry hates fruit.

(See Father Christmas, Presents, Socks)

Saturday

Henry's favourite day of the week – no school, no homework and lots of TV, as long as he gets to the comfy black chair before Peter. Henry's mean old parents always try and spoil it by making him do chores.

(See Chores, Comfy Black Chair, Sweet Day)

School

School definitely isn't one of Henry's favourite places – he hates the lessons, the dinners, and especially his horrible teacher, Miss Battle-Axe. When Henry is King, he'll make it the law that parents, not children, go to school.

(See King Henry the Horrible, Miss Battle-Axe, School Dinners)

School Council President

Henry thinks he'd be an outstanding School Council President. He'd make playtime last five hours and ban vegetables from school dinners. But in the election, he's up against the toughest opponent of all, Moody Margaret.

(See Moody Margaret, School Dinners, Vegetables)

School Dinners

Horrid Henry hates school dinners – the smell, the dinner ladies slopping food on the plates, the stringy stew, blobby mashed potatoes and soggy semolina. Perfect Peter loves school dinners, because they're nutritious and delicious, especially the spinach salads.

(See Spinach)

School Fair

Horrid Henry enjoys the School Fair, doing the raffle and the lucky dip and best of all throwing wet sponges at Miss Battle-Axe on the 'Biff a Teacher' stall. And there's always the chance to win a really great prize at his mum's Treasure Map stall.

(See Walkie-Talkie-Burpy-Slurpy-Teasy-Weasy Doll)

School Play

Miss Battle-Axe directs the all-singing, all-dancing school Christmas play and chooses the parts. Everybody wants to be Joseph or Mary, and nobody wants to be a blade of grass. Henry is chosen to be the innkeeper – and he's determined to make the most of his one word part.

(See Acting, Blade of Grass, Miss Battle-Axe)

School Reports

When they read Horrid Henry's horrible school reports, Henry's parents are always angry. Naturally, Peter's reports are perfect, his work is wonderful, and his parents are always proud and pleased.

(See Perfect Peter)

HENRY'S SCHOOL REPORT

It has been horrible Teaching Henry this year. He is rude, lazy and disruptive. The worst student I have ever taught.

Behaviour: Horrid

English: Horrid

Maths: Horrid

Science: Horrid

P.E: Horrid

PETER'S SCHOOL REPORT

It has been a pleasure teaching Peter this year. He is polite, hard-working and co-operative. The best student I have ever taught.

Behaviour: Perfect

English: Perfect

Maths: Perfect

Science: Perfect

P.E: Perfect

School Trip

Henry's class trip to the Frosty Freeze Ice Cream Factory goes wrong when they discover the factory is closed for the day. Instead, they head to the Town Museum where Henry manages to destroy the only interesting exhibit – but avoids getting the blame.

(Frosty Freeze Ice Cream Factory, Our Town Museum)

Screamin' Demon

A comic – one of Horrid Henry's favourite reads.

(See Comics)

Screaming

When Moody Margaret starts screaming, it's the loudest, longest and most ear-piercing noise anyone has ever heard.

(See Moody Margaret)

Secret Club

Moody's Margaret's club. No boys are allowed. Horrid Henry's Purple Hand Gang is the sworn enemy.

(See Biscuits, Dagger, Mottos, Passwords, Purple Hand Gang, Secret Club Tent, Sour Susan)

Secret Club Tent

The Secret Club's den is a tent in Moody Margaret's back garden, where a stash of biscuits is hidden in a biscuit tin under a blanket. Horrid Henry knows just where to find them.

(See Biscuits, Secret Club)

Shop 'n' Drop

This shop runs a 'Win Your Weight in Chocolate' competition that Greedy Graham wants to enter.

(See Chocolate, Greedy Graham)

Shopping

Horrid Henry hates being dragged around for miles with his mum shopping for clothes – he'd prefer to look at gigantic TVs, computer games, comics, toys and sweets. Except when he manages to persuade Mum to buy him a pair of Root-a-Toot trainers.

(See Root-a-Toot Trainers, Toy Heaven, Zippy's Department Store)

Silly Billy

One of Peter's favourite TV programmes. Silly Billy is a singing goat who thinks he's a clown.

Sing-Along-With-Susie

One of Perfect Peter's top favourite TV programmes.

(See TV)

Singing Soraya

A girl in Horrid Henry's class who bursts into song at any opportunity.

Skeleton Bank

Horrid Henry keeps his pocket money in his skeleton bank. But it's nearly always empty because Henry spends his money on crisps, sweets and comics.

(See Pocket Money)

Skeleton Skunks

A book by Horrid Henry's favourite author, TJ Fizz.

(See TJ Fizz)

Skeleton Stinkbomb

TJ Fizz's latest brilliant book.

(See TJ Fizz)

Skull and Crossbones Biscuit Tin

The special tin containing the precious store of Purple Hand Gang biscuits.

(See Purple Hand Gang)

Skull and Crossbones Flag

The Purple Hand Gang's flag.

(See Purple Hand Gang)

Skullbangers

One of Horrid Henry's favourite bands, famous for their 'Bony Boil' song:

Boils on your fat face
Boils make you dumb.
Chop chop chop 'em off
Stick 'em on your bum!

Sleepovers

Horrid Henry loves sleepovers, but he never gets invited back to the same house more than once. Best sleepovers: eating all the ice cream at Greedy Graham's, breaking all the beds at Dizzy Dave's and staying up all night at Rude Ralph's. Worst sleepovers: at New Nick's where the dogs had chewed up all the pillows; at Stuck-Up Steve's when he tried to scare Horrid Henry to death; and when he got trapped inside a chest during Moody Margaret's sleepover.

(See Greedy Graham, Dizzy Dave, Rude Ralph, New Nick, Stuck-Up Steve, Moody Margaret)

Slimy the Slug

One of Perfect Peter's books – but it's far too scary for bedtime.

(See Sammy the Snuggly Snail)

Smelly Nappy

One of Horrid Henry's most horrible names for Perfect Peter.

(See Baby, Name-Calling)

Smelly Toads

The Purple Hand Gang's password.

(See Passwords)

Snails

At Restaurant Le Posh, Horrid Henry orders snails by mistake – and they taste so thrillingly revolting, he's surprised to find he likes them!

(See Restaurant Le Posh)

Snake Master's Revenge

A cool computer game that Henry likes to play.

(See Computer Games)

Snappy Croc

One of Horrid Henry's bath toys – Henry sends Snappy Croc into battle against his other bath toy, Yellow Duck.

(See Bathtime, Yellow Duck)

Snappy Zappy Critter

Mum and Dad told Horrid Henry that he couldn't have this toy even if he begged for a million years – but Grandma bought him one when she came to stay.

(Grandma, Presents)

Sneering Simone

The sneering presenter of the TV programme, Talent Tigers, who comes to judge the talent show at Horrid Henry's school. Henry is desperate to win with his magician act, Il Stupendioso.

(See Horrid Henry, Il Stupendioso, Talent Tigers)

Snoozie Whoozie

The Snoozie Whoozie is a bunny that giggles you to sleep – it's Perfect Peter's best new toy.

(See Toys)

Socks

Horrid Henry is sick of getting socks every birthday and Christmas. Don't his parents understand? Socks are NOT presents.

(See Presents, Satsumas)

Soggy Sid

Horrid Henry's swimming teacher Soggy Sid is big and mean. He makes Henry go swimming even when he's forgotten his costume and the water is icy cold.

(See Swimming, Thursday)

Sour Susan

The sourest girl in Horrid Henry's class. Sour Susan is Moody Margaret's best friend, but only when she does what she's told. Susan often wonders why she is friends with such a bossy, moody old grouch.

(See Chief Spy, Moody Margaret, Secret Club)

Spaghetti and Meatballs

Horrid Henry's favourite dinner, along with burgers and pizza.

Spelling Tests

When Miss Battle-Axe gives Henry's class a spelling test, he always tries to sit next to Clever Clare so he can copy her answers.

(See Clever Clare)

Spiders

Horrid Henry isn't scared of spiders, and he's delighted when he discovers a babysitter who's terrified of them – Rabid Rebecca, the toughest teen in town.

(See Babysitters, Rabid Rebecca)

Spinach

Perfect Peter loves this vegetable.

(See School Dinners, Vegetables)

Splat!

An album by the Killer Boy Rats, Horrid Henry's favourite band.

(See Killer Boy Rats)

Sports Day

Horrid Henry hates Sports Day because he hardly ever wins a single event. No sweets are allowed – everyone has a refreshing piece of orange instead. If Horrid Henry had his way the school would have a TV-watching day or a chocolate-eating day.

(See Chocolate, Cross Country Run, TV)

Spotless Sam

Perfect Peter's friend, and a member of the Best Boys' Club.

(Best Boys' Club)

Sprouts

Horrid Henry hates sprouts – they are so bitter, stomach-churning and green. His parents try to make him eat them, until Henry finds a perfect sprout-sized drawer to hide them in.

(See Vegetables)

Stinkbombs

With their grisly, gruesome smell, stinkbombs are ideal for attacking Moody Margaret's Secret Club.

(See Intergalactic Samurai Gorillas, Secret Club, Stinky Stinkbomb Kit)

Stinky Stinkbomb Kit

Henry loves his stinkbomb-making kit – it's full of horrible smells, like bad breath, dog poo, rotten eggs, smelly socks, dead fish and sewer stench.

(See Stinkbombs)

Stomping

At dance class, Henry prefers to stomp, like an elephant or a big wild buffalo, and definitely NOT like a raindrop. He loves to dance, just not with other children.

(See Dance Class)

Stone-Age Steven

One of Henry's classmates –
Steven stomps around the classroom and says "Ugg" a lot.
He was inspired by the writer and actor Steven Butler,
who played Horrid Henry on stage.

Strum 'n' Drum

This toy makes as much noise as ten bands playing at once.

(See Toys)

Stuck in the Muck

A brilliant TV show, which Horrid Henry loves.

(See TV)

Stuck-up Steve

Rich Aunt Ruby's son and Horrid Henry's slimy cousin and sworn enemy. Stuck-Up Steve thinks he's better than everyone else and is always bragging about all his brand-new toys and games. He's scared of monsters and he and Henry always try to trick each other.

(See Rich Aunt Ruby)

Supersoaker 2000 Water Blaster

The best water blaster ever!

(See Toys)

Sweet Day

Sweet Day is Saturday – the only day that Mum and Dad let Henry eat sweets. (Peter doesn't really like sweets.)

(See Sweets)

Sweets

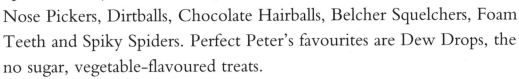

Horrid Henry has loads of favourite sweets – Big Boppers, Blobby Gobbers, Rubber Blubbers, Chocolate Spitballs, Fizzy Fizzers, Gooey Chewies, Nose Pickers, Dirtballs, Chocolate Hairballs, Belcher Squelchers, Foam Teeth and Spiky Spiders. Perfect Peter's favourites are Dew Drops, the no sugar, vegetable-flavoured treats.

(See Hobbies)

Sweet Tweet

The breakfast cereal with a free Gizmo in every box. Horrid Henry and Perfect Peter have eaten mountains of it to build up their Gizmo collections.

(See Collecting, Gizmos)

Swimming

Horrid Henry hates swimming because the water is so cold and wet and soggy and everyone gets badges, except him. He hates Soggy Sid, the swimming teacher too.

(See Excuses, Soggy Sid, Thursday)

Talent Tigers
A TV talent show –
Horrid Henry is a
big fan!
*(See Horrid Henry,
Il Stupendioso,
Sneering Simone)*

Tank Thomas and Tapioca Tina
Co-presenters of Henry's top TV show, Gross-Out.
(See Gross-Out)

Teachers

Horrid Henry likes to show his teachers who's boss. He manages to defeat most of them, but he can't get rid of Miss Battle-Axe.
(See Miss Battle-Axe, Miss Impatience Tutu, Miss Lovely, Miss Marvel, Mr Ninius Nerdon, Mrs Oddbod, Mrs Zip, Soggy Sid)

Tell-Tale Tim

A friend of Perfect Peter's, who is always telling tales.

Terminator Gladiator

Horrid Henry is a huge fan of this TV programme. And he's the proud owner of a Terminator Gladiator toy, a lunchbox, and a Fighting Kit, with a sword, shield, axe and trident. Henry likes him on top of the Christmas tree.
(See Fairies, Toys)

Tetchy Tess

A very bad-tempered babysitter. When Tetchy Tess babysits for Horrid Henry, he floods the bathroom. She never comes again.
(See Babysitters)

Thank You Letters

Perfect Peter writes his thank you letters the moment he finishes unwrapping a present, but Horrid Henry doesn't see why he should waste his precious time saying thank you for presents when he could be reading comics or watching TV.

(See Manners, Presents)

Thursday

The worst day of the week for Horrid Henry because it's his school swimming day. He tries to get out of it every week and his mum calls it 'Thursday-itis'.

(See Soggy Sid, Swimming)

Tidy Ted

One of Perfect Peter's friends, and a member of the Best Boys' Club.

(See Best Boys' Club)

TJ Fizz

The writer of *Ghost Quest, Mad Machines, Skeleton Skunks* and *Ghouls' Jewels* is Horrid Henry's favourite author in the whole world. Henry has read all of TJ Fizz's books and thinks they are even better than Mutant Max comics. And he even got to meet her once…

(See Book Week, Comics)

Toad

A name Henry calls Perfect Peter.

(See Name-Calling)

Tooth Fairy

Horrid Henry is outraged when Perfect Peter loses a tooth and gets a pound from the Tooth Fairy before he does. He comes up with a cunning plan, but the Tooth Fairy turns out to be trickier than he thought…

Tough Toby

The roughest, toughest boy in Henry's class.

Toy Heaven

The best shop in the world! Before Christmas, Henry reads the Toy Heaven catalogue and puts big red X's to mark his present choices and help Santa remember everything he wants.

(See Presents, Toys)

Toys

There are so many brilliant toys that Horrid Henry wants. Why can't his mean, horrible parents buy him them all?

(See Boom-Boom Basher, Curse of the Mummy Kit, Goo-Shooter, Intergalactic Samurai Gorillas, Mega-Whirl Goo Shooter, Shopping, Snappy Croc, Snappy Zappy Critter, Snoozie Whoozie, Stinky Stinkbomb Kit, Strum 'n' Drum, Supersoaker 2000 Water Blaster, Terminator Gladiator, Toy Heaven, Tyrannosaur Dinosaur Roars, Yellow Duck)

TV

Horrid Henry loves watching TV in the comfy black chair, even though his parents only have one teeny tiny telly in the whole, entire house. His favourite TV programmes are: Gross-Out, Hog House, Terminator Gladiator, Cannibal Cook, Rapper Zapper, Robot Rebels, Talent Tigers and Stuck in the Muck. Perfect Peter's favourites are: Daffy and her Dancing Daisies, Manners With Maggie, Nellie's Nursery, Cooking Cuties, Grow and Show, Sammy the Snail, Silly Billy and Sing-Along-With-Susie. When Henry meets the Queen, all he wants to know is how many TVs she has.

(See Cannibal Cook, Comfy Black Chair, Daffy and her Dancing Daisies, Gross-Out, Grow and Show, Hobbies, Hog House, Manners With Maggie, Nellie's Nursery, Silly Billy, Talent Tigers, Terminator Gladiator)

Twizzle Cards

When Henry gets fed up of collecting Gizmos, he starts collecting Twizzle Cards from Scrummy Yummies – there's a free card in every box.

(See Collecting, Gizmos)

Tyrannosaur Dinosaur Roars

A mechanical toy dinosaur that roars, bellows and stomps around, stretching out its claws. Tyrannosaur Dinosaur Roars is the greatest toy ever in the history of the universe! Grandma buys one each for Horrid Henry and Perfect Peter. But who gets the green one and who gets the purple one?

(See Toys)

Underpants

Horrid Henry likes wearing his Driller
Cannibal pants, his Marvin the Maniac
pants, or even his old Gross-Out ones
with the holes and the droopy elastic.
He hates the frilly pink lacy knickers
that Great-Aunt Greta sends him as
a birthday present. And it's even
worse when he accidentally wears
them to school. Peter's favourite
pants are his Daffy and her Dancing
Daisies ones.

(See De-Bagging, Driller Cannibals, Great-Aunt Greta,
Gross-Out, Marvin the Maniac)

Vain Violet

The vainest girl in Horrid Henry's class – Henry likes pulling her pigtails.

Vegetables

Horrid Henry hates vegetables, apart from crisps and ketchup. His parents get so desperate that they promise to take him to Gobble and Go if he eats all his vegetables for five days.
(See Beans, Crisps, Ketchup, Spinach, Sprouts, Virtuous Veggie)

Virtuous Veggie

When Henry's favourite restaurant Gobble and Go closes, a horrible new one called The Virtuous Veggie takes its place. Instead of fantastic pizzas, burgers and chips, there's Spinach Surprise and Broccoli Ice Cream on the menu. Bleccccch!

(See Gobble and Go, Vegetables)

Virtual Classroom

An educational computer game that Henry's parents allow him to play.

(See Computer Games)

Vitamins

The Best Boys' Club password.

(See Passwords)

Vomiting Vera

Prissy Polly and Pimply Paul's baby.
Henry calls her prissy, pimply, stinky,
smelly and wailing! He doesn't want
to see her until she's grown up and
behind bars.

(See Pimply Paul, Prissy Polly)

Vulture Valley

One of the best squares to buy
in the great game of Gotcha.

(See Gotcha)

Walkie-Talkie-Burpy-Slurpy-Teasy-Weasy Doll

The worst Christmas present Horrid Henry has ever received from Great-Aunt Greta. This doll says 'Mama Mama Mama!', 'Baby burp!' and 'Baby slurp!' Henry lives in terror of Rude Ralph or Moody Margaret coming over and finding it. He tries to get rid of it by donating it to the School Fair.

(See Great-Aunt Greta, School Fair)

Walking

Horrid Henry doesn't see the point of walking, especially in the countryside. He's worried his legs might wear down to stumps and his feet might fall off.

(See Countryside)

Weekend

For Horrid Henry this means sleeping in, breakfast in his pyjamas, morning TV, afternoon TV, evening TV, no school and no Miss Battle-Axe for two whole days.

(See Chores, Miss Battle-Axe, Saturday)

Weepy William

The weepiest boy in Henry's class. He's always bursting into tears.

PRRRRRP

Whoopee Cushions

One of Horrid Henry's favourite tricks to embarrass his mum and dad's dinner guests.

(See Guests)

Whoopee for Numbers

One of the dull and boring computer games that Henry's parents buy for him.

(See Computer Games)

Whopper Whoopee

One of Horrid Henry's favourite restaurants.

Wibble Bibble

One of the many nasty names that Horrid Henry has for Perfect Peter.

(See Name-Calling)

Wibble Pants

Another horrid name for Perfect Peter.

(See Name-Calling)

Worm

This is Horrid Henry's favourite name for Peter. He'd love to turn Peter into a worm, and charge everyone 10p to look at him.

(See Lord Worm, Name-Calling)

Yellow Duck

A toy that battles in Henry's bath with Snappy Croc.

(See Bathtime, Snappy Croc)

Zippy Zoe

The fastest girl in Horrid Henry's class – she's always dashing about.

Zippy's Department Store

The department store where Horrid Henry's mum drags him shopping for new clothes. Henry makes such a fuss when his mum tries to buy him a pair of girls' tartan trousers, that she gives up and gets him what he's always wanted.

(See Root-a-Toot Trainers, Shopping)

Zapatron Hip-Hop Dinosaur
One of the many toys on Horrid Henry's wish list.
(See Toys)

Zog
A girl from the future.

Zombie Cat Vampires
One of Horrid Henry's top new bands.

Zombie Vampires
Creatures with big, scary teeth and googly eyes that look like the walking dead.

A List of Everything Horrid

K

L

M

For one lucky winner,

Tony Ross, the genius behind the Horrid Henry illustrations,

will create an original piece of artwork of you with Horrid Henry,

taken from a photograph supplied by you.

HOW TO ENTER

There are 20 gizmos hidden inside the double page illustrations in this book.

Each gizmo looks like this:

Can you find all 20 hidden gizmos?

Once you've found them all, visit the Horrid Henry website at

www.horridhenry.co.uk

to submit your answers.

Closing date: **31st March 2012**

For full terms and conditions, go to

www.horridhenry.co.uk